GARFIELD'S
GUIDE TO DIGITAL CITIZENSHIP

A GARFIELD® GUIDE TO ONLINE ETIQUETTE
Be Kind Online

Garfield created by
JIM DAVIS

Scott Nickel, Pat Craven, and Ciera Lovitt
Glenn Zimmerman, Jeff Wesley, Lynette Nuding, and Tom Howard

Lerner Publications ◆ Minneapolis

This series will help you learn to stay safe and secure online, from playing games to downloading content from the internet. Use the resources and activities in the back of this book to learn more about cybersafety.

This content was created in partnership with the Center for Cyber Safety and Education. The Center for Cyber Safety and Education works to ensure that people across the globe have a positive and safe experience online through their educational programs, scholarships, and research. To learn more, visit www.IAmCyberSafe.org.

Illustrated by Lynette Nuding & Glenn Zimmerman
Written by Scott Nickel, Pat Craven, and Ciera Lovitt
Layouts by Jeff Wesley, Brad Hill, and Tom Howard
Cover pencils by Jeff Wesley
Cover inks & Colors by Larry Fentz

Visit Garfield online at https://www.garfield.com

Lerner Publications Company
An imprint of Lerner Publishing Group, Inc.
241 First Avenue North
Minneapolis, MN 55401 USA

For reading levels and more information, look up this title at www.lernerbooks.com.

Main text font provided by Garfield®.

Library of Congress Cataloging-in-Publication Data

Names: Nickel, Scott, author.
Title: A Garfield guide to online etiquette : be kind online / Scott Nickel, Pat Craven, and Ciera Lovitt, Lunette Nuding, Glenn Zimmerman, and Jeff Wesley.
Other titles: Be kind online
Description: Minneapolis : Lerner Publications, 2020. | Series: Garfield's guide to digital citizenship | Includes bibliographical references and index. | Audience: Ages 7-11. | Audience: Grades 2-3. | Summary: "Nermal gets in trouble with his friend Otto for posting mean photos and comments online. He turns to Dr. Cybrina, cyber safety expert, to learn how to fix his posts and his friendship with Otto"— Provided by publisher.
Identifiers: LCCN 2019028780 (print) | LCCN 2019028781 (ebook) | ISBN 9781541572805 (hardcover) | ISBN 9781541582996 (pdf)
Subjects: LCSH: Online etiquette—Juvenile literature. | Internet—Moral and ethical aspects—Juvenile literature. | Garfield (Fictitious character)—Juvenile literature.
Classification: LCC TK5105.878 .N53 2020 (print) | LCC TK5105.878 (ebook) | DDC 395.5—dc23

LC record available at https://lccn.loc.gov/2019028780
LC ebook record available at https://lccn.loc.gov/2019028781

Manufactured in the United States of America
1-46547-47592-8/12/2019

BE KIND ONLINE!

LET'S CHECK OUT WHAT'S NEW ON **SOCIAL MEDIA!**

OKAY... WE HAVE SOME **BORING** STATUS UPDATES...

"I WORE GREEN SOCKS TODAY"...

I wore green socks today! 😃

"MY PET HAMSTER HAS A COLD"...

My pet hamster has a cold! 😞

"I BOUGHT A BRAND-NEW PENCIL"...

brought a brand new pencil! 😬

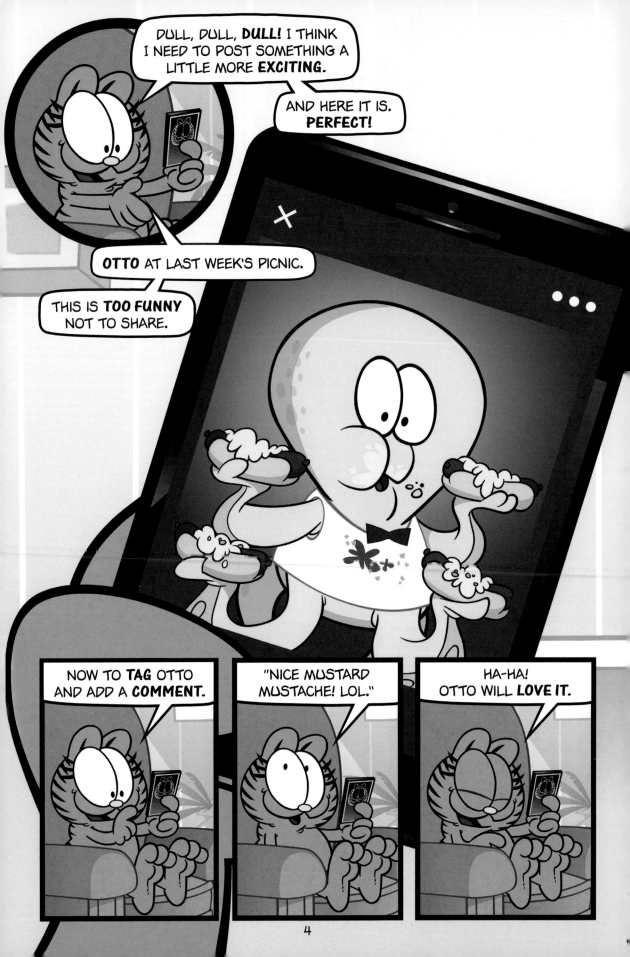

THERE! IT'S **UP!**

WHOA! MY PHONE'S **BLOWIN' UP!**

EVERYONE'S **COMMENTING** ON THE PICTURE OF OTTO.

"OINK! OINK!"

"IS THAT AN OCTOPUS OR A PIG?"

Nice mustard mustache! LOL

OINK! OINK! 😂

Is that an octopus or a pig? 😂

Nice picture, piggy! 😂😂😂

"NICE PICTURE, PIGGY!"

HA! THAT'S A **GOOD ONE!**

"OTTO IS A 'WHALE' OF A GOOD EATER! **LOL.**"

OOH! OR HOW ABOUT **THIS:** "WANT MORE HOT DOGS? OINK ONCE FOR 'YES' LOL!!"

SPEAKING OF **FOOD**, I THINK I COULD USE A LITTLE **SNACK**!

GURGLE!

BREAD...

CHEESE...

SALAMI...

PASTRAMI...

MORE CHEESE, HAM...

OLIVES, PICKLES, ONIONS...

AND JUST A **PINCH** OF MUSTARD!

HEY, GARFIELD! CAN I HAVE A **SANDWICH** TOO?

SORRY, KID!

SPLURT!

ALL I HAVE LEFT IS THE MUSTARD.

SPLURT!

"NICE PICTURE, PORKY! LOL"...

"IS YOUR NAME OTTO OR JUMBO? LOL"...

"THERE'S MORE KETCHUP ON YOUR SHIRT THAN ON THE HOT DOG! LOL"...

"HERE, PIGGY, PIGGY! LOL"...

"#OINKOINK"...

Is that an octopus or a pig?

Nice picture, piggy!

Otto is a 'whale' of a good eater! LOL

Want more hot dogs? Oink once for 'yes' LOL!

Nice picture, Porky! LOL

Is your name Otto or Jumbo? LOL

There's more ketchup on your shirt than on the hot dog! LOL

Here, piggy, piggy! LOL #OinkOink

OH, NO...

THANKS FOR BEING A GREAT FRIEND, NERMAL!

THAT WAS SARCASM, IN CASE YOU COULDN'T TELL.

GOODBYE, NERMAL!

CHA-CLICK! CLICK!

UM, DR. CYBRINA? WE KINDA NEED YOUR **HELP!**

OH, HI, GARFIELD! UM... WHAT'S UP?

IT'S ABOUT **ONLINE SAFETY.**

PERFECT! AS A C.I.S.S.P.— CERTIFIED INFORMATION SYSTEMS SECURITY PROFESSIONAL— I'M ALWAYS ON THE JOB!

I THINK NERMAL MAY HAVE **ACCIDENTALLY** BECOME A **CYBERBULLY.**

THAT'S A **BIG CONCERN.** KIDS NEED TO BE **CAREFUL** ABOUT WHAT THEY **POST** ONLINE, SO THEY DON'T **ACCIDENTALLY** FIND THEMSELVES ON THE **OTHER SIDE** OF **CYBERBULLYING.**

LET ME TALK WITH NERMAL.

HI, DR. CYBRINA. I POSTED WHAT I **THOUGHT** WAS A **FUNNY** PICTURE OF OTTO AND MADE SOME **COMMENTS**.

OTHER PEOPLE COMMENTED TOO. I THOUGHT WE WERE ALL JUST **JOKING** AROUND, BUT I GUESS THE COMMENTS WERE **HURTFUL**.

I THINK I MADE A BIG **MESS**...

DON'T WORRY. WE'LL GET IT **CLEANED** UP!

FIRST THING YOU NEED TO DO IS TAKE THE PHOTO **OFF** THE WEBSITE. UNFORTUNATELY, ONCE THINGS ARE ON THE **INTERNET** THEY WILL **ALWAYS** BE ON THE INTERNET. BUT **REMOVING** THE POST FROM YOUR PAGE WILL HELP **STOP** IT FROM **SPREADING** ANY FURTHER.

DONE!

GOOD. NEXT, WE NEED TO TALK ABOUT **ONLINE ETIQUETTE:** WHAT TO DO AND **NOT** DO ONLINE.

LET'S START WITH **CYBERBULLYING**. BULLYING CAN HAPPEN ON PHONES, SOCIAL MEDIA, GAMES, BLOGS, AND **ANYWHERE** THAT COMMENTS AND PHOTOS CAN BE SENT OR POSTED.

AND WE ALL NEED TO REMEMBER THAT **WORDS** CAN SOMETIMES **HURT**, EVEN IF YOU ARE JUST **JOKING**.

JUST BECAUSE YOU PUT LOL OR A SMILEY FACE AFTER A COMMENT **DOESN'T** MAKE IT OKAY TO POST SOMETHING THAT COULD BE **MEAN OR HARMFUL** WITHOUT IT.

YOU SHOULD **NEVER** POST OR TAG SOMEONE'S PICTURE WITHOUT GETTING THEIR **PERMISSION**— EVEN IF YOU THINK THEY WON'T MIND.

YEAH...

YEAH, I THOUGHT IT WOULD BE **FUNNY** TO POST THAT GOOFY PICTURE OF **OTTO** EATING HOT DOGS.

DID SOMEONE MENTION **HOT DOGS?!**

I DIDN'T DO IT TO BE **MEAN.**

I KNOW YOU DIDN'T. PEOPLE CAN COMMENT INSTANTLY ON SOMETHING ONLINE...

...THAT'S WHY IT'S SO **IMPORTANT** TO THINK **BEFORE** YOU POST OR TAG.

AT OTTO'S HOUSE...

SIGH

OH, WOE IS ME...

THE **INTERNET** RUINED MY LIFE...

Ding-Dong!

WHO COULD THAT BE?

THE MAYOR??!

YES, OTTO.

I'M THE MAYOR, AND I HAVE SOME EXCITING NEWS FOR YOU. I SAW SEVERAL PHOTOS OF YOU ONLINE DOING GOOD DEEDS, SO I WANT TO GIVE YOU...

...THIS CITIZENSHIP AWARD.

WOW! THOSE PICTURES WERE JUST POSTED. THAT WAS FAST!

YES IT WAS, BUT THAT'S THE POWER OF THE INTERNET!

ACTIVITY: BE KIND ONLINE

SAY HELLO TO BISBY, MY CYBERSAFETY BOT.

That's B.I.S.B.— Basic Internet Safety Bot—at your service!

Let's talk online safety and cyberbullying. We're going to learn what's okay to post and what's not okay to post.

PART 1: CYBERSAFE OR CYBERBULLYING

ANSWER THE FOLLOWING QUESTIONS TO SEE IF YOU KNOW WHAT'S OKAY TO SAY OR DO ONLINE AND WHAT'S NOT. WRITE YOUR ANSWERS ON A SEPARATE SHEET OF PAPER.

1. Look at the comments posted about this picture of Arlene. Which are CYBERSAFE? Which are examples of CYBERBULLYING?

A. Arlene, you are awesome!

B. Pink is a great color . . . for a pig! LOL

C. You look happy today.

D. That gap in your teeth looks dumb.

2. Look at the comments posted about this picture of Nermal. Which are *CYBERSAFE*? Which are examples of *CYBERBULLYING*?

A. Nermal, you look like an all-star!

B. I love basketball too.

C. Nermal, you're way too short for basketball. LOL!

D. I didn't know you ever got off the bench ha ha!

3. Look at the comments posted about this picture of Otto. Which are *CYBERSAFE*? Which are examples of *CYBERBULLYING*?

A. Keep the planet green! Yes!

B. Is that the trash that smells, or you? LOL

C. Looks like you belong in the trash pile too!

D. That looks like a lot of work!

4. Look at the comments posted about this picture of Otto. Which are CYBERSAFE? Which are examples of CYBERBULLYING?

A. Are you reading a book called *Otto the Stupid Octopus?* LOL

B. Reading rocks! And so do you!

C. You're a great friend, Otto.

D. Otto, I didn't know you could read! LOL

5. It's fun to forward friendly comments and pictures online, but you need to think about what videos you forward too. Which of these messages are CYBERSAFE? Which are examples of CYBERBULLYING?

A. Can you believe how stupid people are? Watch Jon in this video!

B. Watch this funny video of the mean dog next door getting stuck outside.

C. My favorite team won the game! Go, Panthers! Check out the video of the winning shot!

D. Everyone is sharing my cat video. So cute!

6. True or False? Which of these statements about online activities are TRUE? Which are FALSE?

   A. It's okay to tag someone in a photo without their permission.

   B. It's okay to post personal information about someone you know online as long as it's true.

   C. Make only positive comments or say nothing at all.

   D. You should always tell a parent, guardian, or teacher about a cyberbullying situation, even if you started it.

Congratulations! You have just completed part one. Let's take a look at the answers and see how you did!

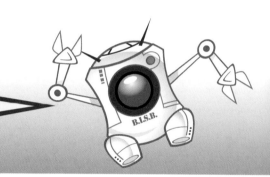

Part 1: Cybersafe or Cyberbullying Answers

IS SOMETHING THAT WAS POSTED ONLINE **CYBERSAFE** OR **CYBERBULLYING?** BELOW ARE THE CORRECT ANSWERS.

1. **Arlene's Photo**

   A. Arlene, you are awesome!
      This is cybersafe!

   B. Pink is a great color . . . for a pig! LOL
      This is cyberbullying!

   C. You look happy today.
      This is cybersafe!

   D. That gap in your teeth looks dumb.
      This is cyberbullying!

2. Nermal's Basketball Photo

A. Nermal, you look like an all-star!
This is cybersafe!

B. I love basketball too.
This is cybersafe!

C. Nermal, you're way too short for basketball. LOL!
This is cyberbullying!

D. I didn't know you ever got off the bench ha ha!
This is cyberbullying!

3. Otto's Picking Up Trash Photo

A. Keep the planet green! Yes!
This is cybersafe!

B. Is that the trash that smells, or you? LOL
This is cyberbullying!

C. Looks like you belong in the trash pile too!
This is cyberbullying!

D. That looks like a lot of work!
This is cybersafe!

4. Otto's Reading Photo

A. Are you reading a book called *Otto the Stupid Octopus*? LOL
This is cyberbullying!

B. Reading rocks! And so do you!
This is cybersafe!

C. You're a great friend, Otto.
This is cybersafe!

D. Otto, I didn't know you could read! LOL
This is cyberbullying!

5. Forwarding Comments or Pictures

A. Can you believe how stupid people are? Watch Jon in this video!
    This is cyberbullying! It's not okay to share because it is hurtful.

B. Watch this funny video of the mean dog next door getting stuck outside.
    This is cyberbullying! It's not okay to share because it is hurtful.

C. My favorite team won the game! Go, Panthers! Check out the video of the winning shot!
    This is cybersafe!

D. Everyone is sharing my cat video. So cute!
    This is cybersafe!

6. True or False

A. It's okay to tag someone in a photo without their permission.
    False

B. It's okay to post personal information about someone you know online as long as it's true.
    False

C. Make only positive comments or say nothing at all.
    True

D. You should always tell a parent, guardian, or teacher about a cyberbullying situation, even if you started it.
    True

> Excellent work! You're on your way to becoming a cybersafety superstar!

> Keep it going!

B.I.S.B.

24

YOU'RE DOING **GREAT!** LET'S TAKE A LOOK AT SOME PICTURES AND COMMENTS THAT COULD BE **POSTED** ONLINE AND MAKE SURE THEY'RE **SAFE AND SECURE**—AND FREE FROM **CYBERBULLYING.**

PART 2: POSTING COMMENTS

LOOK AT THE PICTURES AND READ THE COMMENTS. ON A SEPARATE SHEET OF PAPER, SAY IF EACH COMMENT IS OKAY OR NOT OKAY TO POST, FORWARD, OR SHARE.

1. **Are these comments okay to post?**

A. We both love ice cream!

B. Oink-oink! Garfield is a real ice cream hog. LOL

C. Just chillin'!

2. **Are these comments okay to post?**

A. Planting a tree. Good work!

B. That looks like hard work... but fun!

C. Why don't you dig a hole and bury yourself?!

3. **It's fun to share jokes, but sometimes they are inappropriate or mean. Are these okay to share?**

A. What's a cow's favorite school subject? COWculus!

B. You're so dumb, you think the babysitter sits on babies!

C. What kind of room has no door or windows? A MUSHroom!

PART 2: POSTING COMMENTS ANSWSERS

IT'S IMPORTANT TO KNOW WHAT'S OKAY TO POST AND WHAT'S NOT OKAY TO POST. HERE ARE THE CORRECT ANSWERS.

1. **Are these comments okay to post?**

   A. We both love ice cream!
      This is okay to post!

   B. Oink-oink! Garfield is a real ice cream hog. LOL
      This is not okay to post.

   C. Just chillin'!
      This is okay to post!

2. **Are these comments okay to post?**

   A. Planting a tree. Good work!
      This is okay to post!

   B. That looks like hard work . . . but fun!
      This is okay to post!

   C. Why don't you dig a hole and bury yourself?!
      This is not okay to post.

3. **It's fun to share jokes, but sometimes they are inappropriate or mean. Are these okay to share?**

   A. What's a cow's favorite school subject? COWculus!
      This is okay to share!

   B. You're so dumb, you think the babysitter sits on babies!
      This is not okay to share.

   C. What kind of room has no door or windows? A MUSHroom!
      This is okay to share!

NOODLE ON IT!

DISCUSS YOUR THOUGHTS ON THE QUESTIONS BELOW WITH A FRIEND, OR WRITE THEM ON A SEPARATE SHEET OF PAPER.

1. Have you ever felt unsafe online? Why or why not?

2. Have you ever been to a website with an age limit (minimum age requirement)? Why do you think some websites have age limits?

3. Why is it important to keep passwords private?

4. How do privacy settings help keep you safe?

5. What should you do if a stranger talks to you in real life? What about online?

INTERNET SAFETY TOOLBOX

1. Say only positive comments or say nothing at all.

2. Think before you post or forward pictures and videos.

3. You should always tell an adult about a bullying situation, even if you started it.

4. Never post or share hurtful jokes and comments.

5. Adding "LOL" or a smiley face after a mean comment does not make it okay to post.

6. Delete posts about someone else if they ask you to, even if you think it isn't harmful.

7. Never post or tag a picture of someone without asking their permission first.

8. Block or report mean comments and posts when you see them.

9. Don't share other people's personal information, even if it's true.

10. Make sure your profiles are set to private.

YOU DID GREAT! REMEMBER, IT'S IMPORTANT TO BE KIND ONLINE. WHAT YOU SAY CAN HURT OTHER PEOPLE, EVEN IF YOU ARE JUST KIDDING.

B.I.S.B.

B.I.S.B.

Use this tool kit as a guide when using social media and the internet in general.

Congratulations! You are officially an Online Safety Superstar Extraordinaire!

GLOSSARY

citizenship: being part of a community

cyber: related to computers and the internet

cyberbullying: using electronic communication to bully another person

etiquette: appropriate behavior

information systems: systems that interpret and organize information

social media: forms of electronic communication through which users create online communities for sharing information, ideas, personal messages, and other content

tag: to identify someone, usually in a photo

FURTHER INFORMATION

Anton, Carrie. *Digital World: How to Connect, Share, Play, and Keep Yourself Safe*. Middleton, WI: American Girl, 2017.

Being Safe on the Internet.
https://kidshelpline.com.au/kids/issues/being-safe-internet

5 Internet Safety Tips for Kids
https://www.commonsensemedia.org/videos/5-internet-safety-tips-for-kids

Hubbard, Ben. *My Digital Safety and Security*. Minneapolis: Lerner Publications, 2019.

Lyons, Heather, and Elizabeth Tweedale. *Online Safety for Coders*. Minneapolis: Lerner Publications, 2017.

Secure Password Tips from ConnectSafely.org
http://www.safekids.com/tips-for-strong-secure-passwords/

Explore more about Cyber Safety at www.IAmCyberSafe.org

INDEX